Feb. 14, 2020

To Cal,

A special story for an amazing Grandson.

Happy Valentine's Day!

Love you to the Moon and back!

Mae Mae & Pep

Beau's Bayou Treasure

Beau's Bayou Treasure

By Rosalind & Maggie Bunn

Illustrated by Michael P. White

"How sweet it is to be on the bayou..."

Rosalid Bunn

RIVER
ROAD
PRESS

New Orleans
2020

ISBN: 978-1-941879-28-3

The name and logo for "River Road Press" are trademarks of River Road Press LLC and are registered with the U.S. Patent and Trademark Office.

For information regarding permission to reproduce selections from this book, write to Permissions, River Road Press LLC, PO Box 125, Metairie, Louisiana 70004.

For information on other River Road Press titles, please visit www.riverroadpress.com.

Printed in Korea

Published by River Road Press
PO Box 125
Metairie, LA 70004

To Papoo and his treasure hunters,
Tyler and Lane.—RB & MB

To my wife, Traci, and to my daughter,
Madeline, who holds the map to my heart.
To Patty Scott and the Cook family—Frank,
Niki, Zoe, and Annabelle—who point me in
the right direction.
And to all grandparents.
The bond you share with a child is the true
treasure.—MPW

Beau was so excited
  he could hardly sleep.
The map held clues
  to the treasure he would seek.

The bayou flickered
with lightning bugs aglow.
Waiting for daylight
is so hard, you know!

When morning came,
off Beau would go
On a hunt for things
Papoo's map might show.

When the sun rose,
his gear was packed and ready;
The canoe on the bank
waited sure and steady.

Beau paddled the canoe
as the sun shimmered;
Through the bald cypress,
the dark water glimmered.

The first stop on the map
was a big hollow log
Where a turtle sunbathed
just over the bog.

The old turtle asked,
 "Where are you going?"
Beau was surprised.
 "Nowhere! I'm just rowing."

"Snap! Snap! Little boy,
 don't make me upset.
Legend says only thunder
 can make me forget."

"I am exploring the places
   Papoo used to go.
I hope to find treasure
   among the palmetto."

"Oh yes!" Turtle said.
   "There is treasure to be found.
Keep rowing, Beau.
   Look all around."

Beau looked at the map,
 and he could see
Close to the bank
 was an old pecan tree.

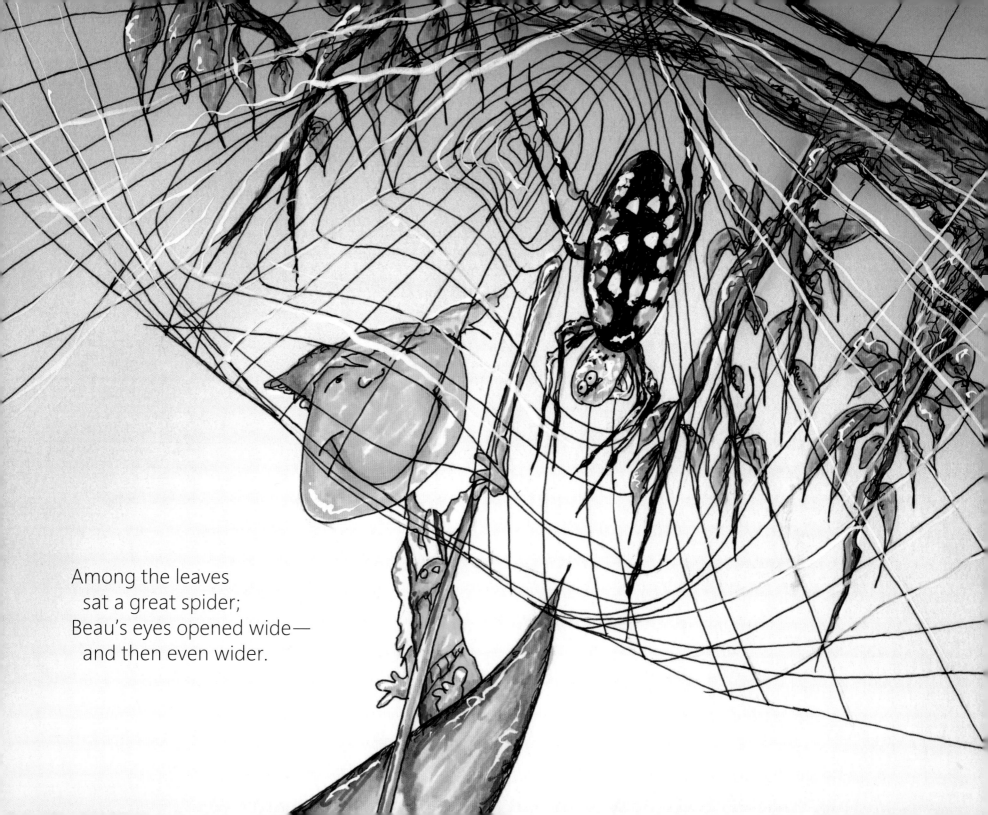

Among the leaves
sat a great spider;
Beau's eyes opened wide—
and then even wider.

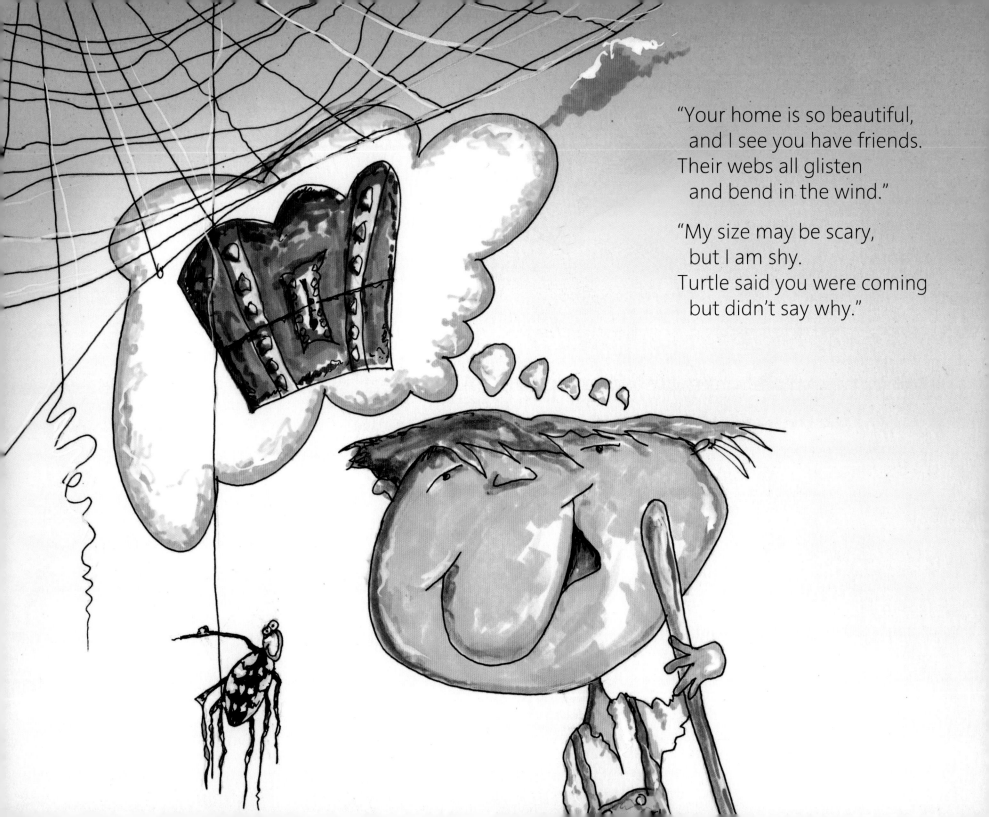

"Your home is so beautiful,
   and I see you have friends.
Their webs all glisten
   and bend in the wind."

"My size may be scary,
   but I am shy.
Turtle said you were coming
   but didn't say why."

"I'm looking for treasure. The map shows it's near.
Am I getting closer?" Beau leaned in to hear.

"Oh yes!" Spider said. "There is treasure to be found.
Keep rowing, Beau. Look all around."

Moss tickled Beau's face
  on his way through the trees.
The map showed fish
  circling tall cypress knees.

As he cast the line,
  there was a tug then a splash.
A huge catfish landed
  in the canoe with a crash.

Beau knew the catfish had seen down below.
Was there treasure at the bottom?
  He just had to know.

"Oh yes!" Catfish said.
  "There is treasure to be found.
Keep rowing, Beau. Look all around."

Beau jumped off his seat as a voice growled from behind:
"That's my lunch! Give it back; it's mine!"

The boy turned around; he saw teeth and a gator.
Throwing the catfish his way, he said, "See ya later."

Whew! That was a close one,
    and as Beau looked around,
Each little frog on the tree
    called its own croaking sound.

It was time to go home
    when he heard the frogs sing,
To share his adventures
    on the old front porch swing.

As Beau paddled back home,
   he pondered his day,
The creatures he'd met,
   all he'd seen on the way.

Where was the treasure?
He just didn't know.
But his love for the bayou
continued to grow.

He spotted a pelican flying in from the coast.
The big bird perched on his bow like a post.

He said, "Thanks for the ride.
 Come back any time.
It's peaceful here,
 and the weather is fine."

The bright light in the distance
was all Beau could see.
Papoo sat on the front porch
waiting patiently.

As the daylight faded
to a dark, dark gray,
Beau told Papoo
of his adventures this day.

"Did you find any treasure?"
Papoo winked as a hint.
Beau then understood
what Papoo really meant.

"Oh yes!" Beau said.
"I rowed and rowed
and looked all around.
Right in my backyard
the treasure was found."

Did You Know?

Bayou Petite Prairie is a slow-moving stream that meanders through St. Landry Parish in southern Louisiana. It provides a home for many animals, from fish and small birds to bobcats and alligators.

The brown pelican is Louisiana's state bird, and it cannot resist the great fishing on the bayou. A pelican will dive into the water and scoop fish into its mouth. Its expandable throat pouch can hold three gallons of water while its stomach can hold only one.

Snapping turtles spend most of their lives in the water. They can hold their breath for up to fifty minutes before they must surface for air. They use their bright red tongues as a lure for fish and frogs in the murky water. They have a strong bite, so you don't want to get too close!

There are many different species of spiders on the bayou. The golden silk orb-weaver, also known as the banana spider, weaves a golden web that can span several yards and is strong enough to capture large prey like cicadas. The body of this spider is orange in color, but its head is white with black markings and resembles a skull.

Catfish are meat-eating bottom feeders. Their "whiskers" act as a spiky defense mechanism against predators. Some species of catfish are nocturnal, resting all day but active at night. They are hardy fish that can withstand temperatures just above freezing all the way up to one hundred degrees Fahrenheit.

Alligators love the muddy, swamp-like ecosystem that is the bayou. They can live as long as fifty years and weigh as much as one thousand pounds!